PUCKSTER'S FIRST HOCKEY TOURNAMENT

BY LORNA SCHULTZ NICHOLSON
ILLUSTRATED BY KELLY FINDLEY

After months of waiting, Puckster and his pals were playing in the Great Hockey Challenge!

"Wow," squeaked Charlie, staring at the huge whiteboard set up just inside the arena doors. "There are so many teams."

Puckster pointed to Team Canada's name. "Our first game is in two hours. And we play again this afternoon."

"We might play tomorrow too – in the gold medal game," said Manny.

"First, we have to win both games today," said Puckster.

Roly patted his stomach. "I'm so nervous. I need food." He sniffed. "I smell hot dogs. I *looove* hot dogs."

Just before the game, Roly ordered one hot dog. He loaded it with ketchup, mustard, relish, and onions and ate it as he walked to the dressing room.

Finally, it was time! After a quick cheer for luck, Team Canada stepped on the ice to face the Toronto Tornadoes. As the players took their positions, Roly put his water bottle on top of his net and flipped his goalie mask down.

The referee dropped the puck and Puckster batted at it.

A Tornado picked it up and swirled toward Roly, winding up for a slap shot.

Roly watched as the puck flew over his shoulder and into the net. He hung his head.

Puckster patted his back. "Don't worry. It's just one goal."

Once again, Puckster lined up at centre ice. The referee dropped the puck and this time Puckster nabbed it. He sent it to Sarah and she wheeled down the ice.

"I'm open!" Charlie called, as he zipped over the blue line.

Sarah flipped the puck to Charlie and he smacked it into the net. Team Canada was on the scoreboard! Shortly after, Puckster popped in a rebound for another goal.

When the buzzer sounded, ending the period, the score was 2-1 for Team Canada.

Neither team scored in the second period. In the third, Sarah scored with a snap shot. A Tornado player won the next face-off and skated toward Roly. Roly's legs shook. He crouched to make the save, but the Tornado scored. It was now 3-2 with just three minutes left!

"We can do this, guys," Puckster said. "No more shots on net!"

Team Canada skated and skated. When the final buzzer sounded, the score was still 3-2. Puckster and his pals gave each other a round of high fives.

After the game, Team Canada found a quiet spot in the arena where they could rest. They listened to music and played video games. And they all ate the healthy sandwiches that Puckster had made.

Just before the second game, Roly's stomach started to flip-flop, so he headed to the snack bar. "I need to eat again," he called over his shoulder.

He ordered two plates of french fries with gravy.

"I *looove* french fries," he said.

Team Canada's second game was against the Vancouver Vipers.

The Vipers slinked up and down, darting and weaving. They were fast, but they weren't very accurate. Roly didn't have to make any saves.

Puckster scored in the first period. Manny scored in the second. At the start of the third period the score was 2-0 for Team Canada.

But from the face-off, Charlie got the puck caught in his tail. A Viper slithered by and stole the puck. Roly tried to get into his crouch, but his tummy felt sick. The Viper shot low and the puck skidded between Roly's legs.

"Let's hold them off!" shouted Puckster. By skating hard, Team Canada did just that. They won the game 2-1.

Puckster smiled. "Tomorrow, we play the Russian Boars."

The team met at the arena the next morning. Roly headed straight for the snack bar and ordered three pieces of pizza.

"You don't have to eat that pizza," said Puckster. "I brought apples, bananas, and oranges."

"But I *looove* pizza." Roly gobbled all three pieces down in a hurry.

On the bench, Puckster clapped his hands with excitement. "Our first gold medal game!" he said.

All the players cheered – except Roly. He put his hand on his stomach and groaned.

The whistle blew, starting the game. Puckster grabbed the puck and sped straight toward the Russian Boars' net. When he saw Francois fly past on his wing, he passed the puck to him. Francois nailed a shot that zinged into the net, setting off the red goal light.

The next time the puck dropped, a Russian player pounced on it and barrelled toward Roly. Manny tried to block the Russian, but the Boar pushed by and swiped at the puck. Roly's stomach hurt so badly that he couldn't bend over. The puck sailed into the net.

The Boars then added two more goals. At the end of the period, the score was 3-1 for Russia.

At the break, Roly skated to the bench and lay down. "I don't feel good," he said. "I can't play."

"What are we going to do?" Charlie squeaked.

"We need a goalie," said Sarah.

No one spoke. Finally, Francois said, "I could try."

Piece by piece, Francois put on Roly's giant goalie gear. The pads went up to Francois's waist. The chest protector hung to his knees.

The referee blew his whistle and Francois plodded to the net.

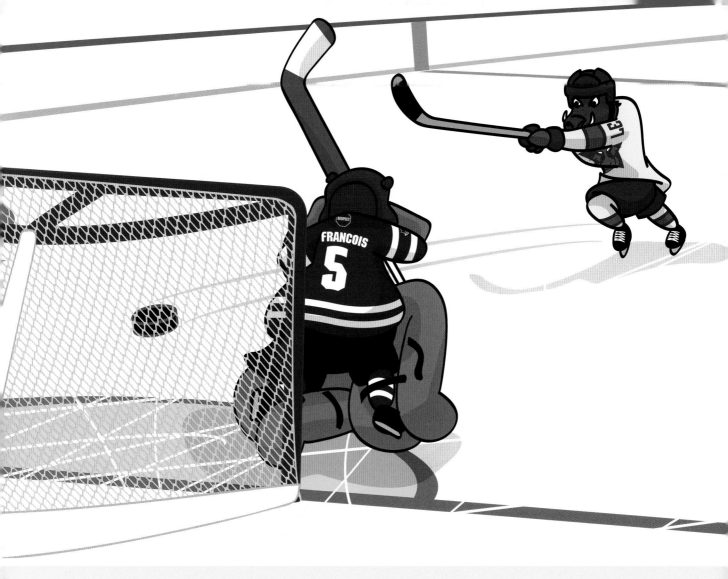

Off the face-off, a Russian picked up the puck and raced toward the net. He wound up and shot.

Francois raised the huge blocker so it covered his face. The red goal light blinked on. It was another goal for the Boars.

"We can do this!" said Puckster.

On the next play, Puckster passed to Sarah. She weaved down the ice and sunk a wrist shot.

Then Manny blasted a slap shot for a goal.

At the end of the second period, the score was 4-3. But Puckster and his pals were exhausted!

Puckster skated to the bench. "You have to help us, Roly," Puckster said. "We can't win without you." Roly nodded and suited back up.

Halfway through the third period, Manny boomed a wrist shot from the hash marks. The puck beat the Russian goalie. It was now a tie game!

Ten minutes later, the buzzer sounded. The game was going into sudden death overtime!

Roly skated to the bench, holding his stomach. "I can't do this anymore."

"But we need you," replied Puckster.

"Don't let us down," Francois pleaded.

Roly sighed and skated to the net as both teams took their positions.

The referee dropped the puck. Barely a second later, two Russians raced toward Roly. The puck carrier faked a pass and then shot. Roly slid across the net, whipped his glove in the air, and made a spectacular save. The fans cheered!

On the next play, Puckster got the puck. He skated toward the Russian net and rifled a shot. The red light glowed. Puckster had scored and his team had won the game!

Puckster and his pals threw their gloves in the air.

The Team Canada players smiled as they got their gold medals.
Puckster turned to Roly. "I'm glad you went back in the net."
Roly smiled and kissed his medal. "So am I," said Roly. "Thanks, Puckster."

PUCKSTER'S TIPS:

It's important to eat properly before every game.

Don't ever give up – even if you're playing as a goalie and you've let in lots of goals.

When you're first learning to play hockey, try every position.

PUCKSTER'S HOCKEY TIP:

To take a **wrist shot,** start with the puck behind you.
As you pull it forward, **shift your weight from
your back leg to your front leg.**
Follow through, pointing your stick at the target.

Good luck!

 24